SHADOWS OF THE PAST

ISBN: 979-8-9911532-7-0

SHADOWS OF THE PAST

By Tressym

HezzieMae

INDEPENDENT BOOK PUBLISHING

DULUTH, MN

CONTENTS

Chapter One 1

Chapter Two 9

Chapter Three 15

Chapter Four 25

Chapter Five 31

Interlude – Ten Years Ago 37

Chapter Six 41

Chapter Seven 53

Chapter Eight 67

Chapter Nine 73

Interlude 83

Chapter Ten 89

Chapter Eleven 101

About the Author 105

CHAPTER ONE

Today was Elysia's fiftieth birthday, even though she only looked about fifteen. Elysia was in her room, getting ready to leave. The room was dark, with only a few candles for light. The lack of light didn't matter, as Elysia could see in the dark. In the middle of the room was a large four-poster bed, and bookshelves lined the walls. Elysia would miss home, but she would be back soon.

"Elysia," she heard her mother call from downstairs, "Are you ready yet?"

Elysia sighed, "I'm coming."

Elysia turned to look at herself in the mirror. She was wearing a dark blue traveling dress and black leather boots. She grabbed a ribbon and tied back her long black and silver hair, revealing her pointed ears. Her silver eyes shone in the reflection of the moonlight coming through the window.

When she was ready, Elysia walked down the stairs. Her family waited in the main living room. Her mother, Sylvena, walked over to her.

"Are you excited to go?" Sylvena said.

Elysia smiled. "I can't wait!"

"Why can't I come too?" her younger sister, Zia, asked.

"It's not your birthday, Zia," Malvina said.

Malvina was the oldest of the sisters. She had silver hair like their mother, unlike Zia, who had black hair like their father. All of the sisters had the same silver eyes, however.

"It's still not fair," Zia said, shooting a glare at Elysia.

Malvina ignored her. "I hope you have a good time in the mortal realm," she said. "I will warn you, though, it's not as glamorous as you may think."

Elysia and her family were Fey, and Elysia had never been out of the Feywild before. The Fey, also known as Faeries, Fair Folk, or the Sidhe, were varied—from sprites and pixies, tiny humanoid creatures with wings, to the high Fey, like Elysia's family, who closely resembled their cousins, the Elves, to mind-twisting monstrosities made of nightmares that lived in the farthest reaches of the forest. For all their differences, the Fey shared their innate ability for magic, the inability to tell direct lies, an inherent weakness to iron, and a centuries-long lifespan—if they weren't immortal, as most of the high Fey were.

The Feywild was the realm of the Fey, divided into two courts. The Summer Court was ruled by Titania, queen of the Seelie Fey. The Winter Court's monarch was Mab, queen of the Unseelie Fey. The two queens historically did not get along, and members of the two courts interacted sparingly, sometimes forging grudging alliances. Aside from the two main courts, there was also a small, unaffiliated group known as the Wyldfae. The Wyldfae mostly minded their own business, preferring to stay out of the elaborate games of four-dimensional chess that were the schemes of the courts. Both courts, including the Wyldfae, were simultaneously feared and spoken of as wondrous places of magic in the human world.

Elysia looked to her sisters. "I'll miss you, but it will be exciting to go on an adventure. Don't worry, Malvina, Father and I will be safe. And Zia, I'm sure you'll get to go when you're older."

Zia crossed her arms and looked annoyed. Elysia walked outside, her mother and sisters following her. It was snowing lightly that night, and there was frost on the trees surrounding their house. Some of the trees were completely covered in ice if they weren't actually made of ice. The house was made of stone and had trees growing close to it. Even though it was over three stories tall, it almost looked like a part of the forest itself. Elysia ran over to her father, who was preparing the teleportation circle. Her father, Wilfred, was a vampire with black hair and dark brown eyes. He was carefully arranging a collection of small objects on the ground into a circle.

"Is the portal ready yet?" Elysia asked.

"Almost," Wilfred said. "Malvina just needs to activate it."

Malvina walked over to the circle of various bones, gemstones, and other oddities on the snowy ground. She summoned her wizard's staff, a long piece of unnaturally white bone with a smoky grey sphere on top. Elysia knew that the bone was from a demon Malvina had killed during her adventuring days, and she had made a powerful conduit for magic from it. The grey sphere seemed to be filled with smoke, giving Elysia a headache when she looked at it for too long.

Malvina was over two hundred and seventy years old and had lots of experience fighting with her magic, which was centered around dreams and time. She was the most skilled member of the family and the only one who used advanced portal magic. Malvina drew her staff around the circle, and the objects disappeared. A circle formed on the ground, the colour of grey smoke.

Elysia took one last look around at the big stone house in the middle of a winter forest. She turned and gave Malvina a hug.

"I'll contact you when we get to Stonewood," she said. "We'll be back soon."

Stonewood was the city in the mortal realm that they were traveling to. Elysia bid her mother and sisters goodbye, took her father's hand, and they stepped through the portal. Malvina was skilled with portal magic, so there was little indication that they had even passed into another plane. It was just like stepping through a doorway.

Elysia looked around the forest she had been transported into. She was disappointed. All the books she had read said that the mortal realm was full of adventure and wonder. But all she saw was a normal forest, more dull than normal, even. It wasn't winter here, but late fall. She saw a squirrel in a tree. It wasn't even glowing or glittering, just a strange, dull-grey squirrel. All of the colours around her seemed less vibrant as well, and the leaves of the trees were more off-red-brown rather than vibrant red or orange. Instead of the natural magic of the Feywild, this place just seemed… boring.

"What do you think?" Wilfred asked her.

"It's so… dull," Elysia responded. "I can barely feel any magic in this place."

"That's because there *is* barely any magic. The Feywild is the opposite of the mortal world. A more magical mirror of it. Just as the Shadowfell is a bleaker representation."

"I know that," Elysia said, rolling her eyes at the lecture. "But I was still hoping it would be more interesting. Which direction is Stonewood?"

"You seem excited," Wilfred laughed. "Don't worry, we'll head there soon. Let's set up camp first so we can get a fresh start in the morning."

Elysia nodded and opened her extradimensional storage space. Elysia was a shadow sorcerer like Wilfred. Instead of using a wide range of magic like wizards, sorcerers specialized in one type of magic they inherited from their parents or an ancient bloodline. Vampires naturally had a strong affinity for shadows, and being half-vampire gave Elysia a stronger connection to shadow, making her more powerful than the average shadow sorcerer.

When she opened her pocket dimension, a three-dimensional sphere manifested in front of her, drawing substance from the shadows of the trees around her. Elysia reached into the sphere and brought out a small wooden figurine of a hut. When the command word was spoken, it would transform into a normal-sized building. Sylvena had given it to her before she had left.

Elysia and Wilfred walked a short distance to a nearby clearing in the woods. Elysia set the figurine down on the ground and spoke the command word. Nothing happened. Elysia spoke the command word again. Nothing happened.

Elysia looked at her father. "Why isn't it working?"

Wilfred frowned and picked up the figure. "That's strange," he said. "I'll check to make sure there's nothing strange going on magically."

Wilfred waved his hand, likely to summon shadows to investigate. Nothing happened. Wilfred looked confused for a moment. Then, realization dawned on his face.

"Elysia, get out of the clearing," he said suddenly.

"Why?" she asked. "What's wrong?"

"It's an antimagic circle," Wilfred said. "I didn't sense it before. Something strange is going on."

As soon as he finished speaking, the forest was flooded with a blinding light.

CHAPTER TWO

Elysia instinctively tried to summon her shadows to block out the bright light, but the antimagic field blocked her magic. She heard shouting and the sound of armour clinking. Suddenly, the light vanished, and she could see again. Elysia saw four humans wearing plate mail armour and carrying greatswords. They had surrounded Wilfred. Elysia backed away, trying to disappear into the forest, when she ran into someone.

It was a tall human man with light brown hair. He wore different, more intricate armor than the others but had the same greatsword. Elysia attempted to use her shadows to make herself invisible and run away, but he grabbed her arms and put manacles on her wrists. Elysia immediately knew the manacles were made of iron. Iron blocked the magic of the Fey and was extremely painful when they tried to use magic against it.

"You're not going anywhere," the human said, walking her back toward the clearing. The other humans still surrounded Wilfred, their greatswords out and ready to attack.

Elysia was nervous. Normally, these humans wouldn't stand a chance against Wilfred, but the sudden light had been infused with radiant magic, the opposite of shadow, and had weakened him significantly.

"I found the girl trying to run away," Elysia's captor said. "You can kill him now."

"No!" Elysia said. "Why are you doing this? You don't even know who we are! Let me go!"

She spoke in Common, the language that the humans were using. It was highly unlikely that they knew the Fey language.

The human chuckled, "I know who you are. That's why we're here. Evil undead like your father over there can't be allowed to continue existing."

He gestured to his companions. "I said get rid of him."

Two of the humans advanced on Wilfred, the one on the left feinting an attack so the other could restrain him. With the two humans restraining him, the third advanced. Wilfred struggled for a moment, but he gave up quickly. He must have realized that the humans had the upper hand in this situation, and trying to get away was pointless. Instead of using their greatsword, the human lifted a wooden stake from their other hand. Elysia was terrified. They really were going to kill her father. These humans must be vampire hunters.

The human walked over to Wilfred and moved to stab him in the heart with the stake. Right before the stake hit Wilfred, he looked directly at Elysia. He seemed about to say something, but the human drove the stake into his heart. Wilfred looked surprised for a moment, as though he couldn't believe he had just gotten stabbed.

Elysia watched as the light left his eyes. Even though she knew it was only a few seconds, the moment seemed to stretch into eternity. Eventually, Wilfred's body went limp, and the humans dragged him away.

Elysia forgot all about the human holding her captive. Her father had just died. No, not just died, but been killed. By these humans. She blinked away tears. She wouldn't cry in front of these humans. They didn't deserve to get a reaction out of her.

Some of her grief disappeared at that thought, replaced with cold rage. She would get revenge, she decided. She would kill these humans who had taken her father away. Elysia turned toward the human next to her.

"You're going to die," she said, perfectly calm. She was just stating a fact. That was what would happen. He would die at her hand.

"Yeah, sure," the man scoffed, although Elysia could tell she had unnerved him. "What are you going to do, kid? Use your unholy magic to get your revenge? I don't think so."

He glanced at her iron manacles. "You can't do anything. You're our prisoner now."

"Let's go," one of the other humans said. He was younger than the one who had captured her and looked nervous. "Bring the body. Time to go back to camp. We got our job done."

Two of the humans grabbed Wilfred's body and started off into the forest. Elysia had no choice but to follow them.

Hours later, after night had fallen, Elysia and the humans arrived at the humans' camp. There were five tents in a clearing, surrounding a large pile of sticks and logs, with torches around the perimeter. The two humans carrying Wilfred's body walked over to the pile of sticks and threw Wilfred on it.

"Light 'em up," the leader of the humans said.

Oh no, they're going to burn him. Elysia thought. No vampire could come back from the dead if their body were burned. Elysia watched as one of the humans grabbed a torch and lit the pile of sticks and logs on fire. The fire engulfed the logs and Wilfred's body. Elysia stared numbly at the bonfire. The lead human standing behind her spoke to one of his companions.

"Keep a guard on her at all times," he said. "I'll take the first shift. Keep the fire going til' it's ash, Larry."

"Yes, Jim Bob, sir," one of the humans said, presumably Larry.

Elysia noted that he had acted nervous earlier. Maybe she could use that against him later. Jim Bob tied her manacles to a tree with rope near the circle of tents, then stood guard nearby, leaning against a tree. Elysia couldn't believe the situation she was in. Had her father, a centuries-old vampire, been killed by a *human* named *Jim Bob*?

Nothing in this situation added up. She needed a plan.

"So, Jim Bob," Elysia said after sitting down next to the tree, "What are you, a bunch of humans, going around murdering people for?"

"That wasn't a murder," he said. "It was an execution. All undead are evil and unholy and deserve to be eradicated from this land. Righteousness and divine power will prevail."

Elysia already hated him even more. "Why am I still alive then?"

"I don't answer questions from prisoners," he said and turned away from her.

Interesting, they needed her alive for some reason then. Elysia was frustrated that she couldn't get more information from Jim Bob. She needed to know more before she could do anything.

She still needed to find a way around those cursed iron manacles. She wasn't physically strong enough to take out one of the guards. Could she somehow get Jim Bob to come closer and steal the keys from him? She couldn't cut the rope tying her to the tree without the humans noticing, either. If only she could use her magic, then she could fix all her problems. Eventually, her mind strayed away from her problems, and she fell asleep.

CHAPTER THREE

When Elysia woke up, it was almost dawn. The wind had picked up, and the fall leaves were being tossed around. The bonfire had burned away during the night, and all traces of Wilfred were gone. The humans had even covered the ash with dirt.

Elysia noticed that her guard was gone. She looked around and saw all the humans clustered in a group at the other end of the camp. None of them were wearing their armour, and they all had backpacks on. Most of the tents had been taken down as well. That was stupid of them, leaving her without a guard and out of sight.

Elysia tried to gather the shadows around her so she could go invisible and sneak away, but she immediately felt a burning pain where her wrists were tied to the tree. She had forgotten about the iron manacles. She looked down at her hands. She couldn't see anything.

It had *worked?* Trying to use her magic was just as painful as she had heard it would be, but she wasn't supposed to be able to use her magic when her skin was in contact with iron. It was like that for all of the Fey. But apparently not her. It was more difficult to use her magic, though.

Elysia let her magic fade away before the humans noticed, and she became visible again as the pain faded. Larry split off from the group a few minutes later and walked toward her. She noticed he was wearing a backpack like the others.

"Ah, you're awake," he said. "Good, we're going to leave soon."

"Is that what you were all discussing over there?" Elysia asked. "Where are we going?"

"Look, kid," Larry said, "I don't know. I'm sure it's not your fault we were asked to do all this. I just go where the boss says."

Elysia was getting sick of being called 'kid.' She was much older than any of these humans, even if she didn't look like it. They clearly knew nothing about the Fey. It wasn't her fault her people aged slowly.

"So you and your little group of fanatics were hired by someone?" Elysia asked.

Larry cursed, "I said too much. You're getting a different guard before we leave."

He started walking back toward the group but stopped dead in his tracks. The shadow of the tree had suddenly become three-dimensional, wrapping around him like pitch-black tentacles. Elysia moved her hand, and the shadows engulfed Larry's head, choking him before he could cry out for help. Using her magic through the iron hurt, but Elysia had trained in pain management. Elysia commanded the shadows to lower Larry's body to the ground.

Elysia had the shadows pull Larry's body closer, and she used them to root through his backpack. She found what she was looking for. A knife and a set of keys, among the other supplies he had. The shadow tendril used the knife to cut the rope and then to unlock her manacles. With the iron gone, it was amazing to feel the magic in the air again and the presence of every shadow in the area, all of it ready to obey her command.

Elysia summoned her Shadow Blade. It was a thin, curved sword made up entirely of shadows. It looked like a cross between a shortsword and a scimitar. When she walked, small streams of shadows pulled away from it like smoke. Blade in hand, Elysia strode into the camp, her shadows trailing in her wake.

When Elysia arrived at the other side of the camp, Jim Bob's lackeys had surrounded him, ready to defend their leader.

"Where is Larry?" one of them asked. "How did you escape?"

Elysia ignored him and spoke directly to Jim Bob. "Who hired you?" she asked.

He looked her directly in the eye. "I will take that secret to my grave," he said.

Elysia shrugged, "So be it."

Shadows shot up from the ground, catching all three other humans and ensnaring them. They immediately struggled, trying to free themselves. The shadows around their necks tightened, and they stopped struggling, getting the message. Jim Bob shot a glance at his allies. He was nervous.

"You don't want to fight me," he said. "Just let my friends go, and we won't have to hurt you."

"I'm not the one that should worry about getting hurt," Elysia said.

Then she rammed her blade into the side of one of Jim Bob's companions. Jim Bob's eyes widened, and then his expression hardened.

"They wanted you alive," he said, "but I guess bringing back a body is better than nothing at all."

He drew his greatsword, and the blade lit up with divine light. "Time to purge some evil," Jim Bob said.

And then the battle began.

Jim Bob let out a battle cry and rushed toward Elysia, his sword aimed at her head. She easily dodged out of the way and slashed him in the side with her weapon. The wound turned black, and a line of shadow pulled away from Jim Bob, disappearing into Elysia's hand. Her silver eyes glittered, and Jim Bob stumbled away from her.

"What did you do to me?" he asked, concern creeping into his words.

"I drained some of your magic," she said. "Half vampire, remember?" She made a face. "Your holy magic tastes weird, though. Too much divine righteousness."

Elysia didn't use this ability often and almost never while fighting any of the Fey. Advertising any unusual abilities in the Winter Court wasn't a very good idea. She didn't want some crazed scientist wanting to study her, a jealous rival deciding she was too dangerous to be left alive, or any other countless bad situations. She wasn't worried about revealing this ability to Jim Bob. It didn't matter because he would be dead soon anyway. Besides, anything that unnerved and scared Jim Bob was worth it.

Jim Bob glared, "You are evil, just like your father, and must be removed from existence."

He tried to swing at her again, but she was much quicker than him and dodged out of the way. Jim Bob clearly thought he was a skilled swordsman, but he didn't have the decades of experience that Elysia had. He made too many mistakes, and it was easy for Elysia to sidestep his attacks.

Honestly, Elysia had hoped that Jim Bob *would* be skilled. Then, it would have made sense for him to defeat Wilfred. The thought of her father made her more angry at Jim Bob, and Elysia stepped closer, her shadows encroaching toward him. The shadows covered almost the entire camp now, letting almost no light through. The wind started to pick up.

"Really?" she said. "I'm the evil one? What about all of the people you have killed, all of the families you have ripped apart? You say that you cast a holy light, but you avoid the long shadow that follows in your wake."

Jim Bob stared at her, fear on his face. Elysia knew how she must have looked, standing before him, her black and silver hair flying around her face, her eyes shining in the dim light. Her sword was held in front of her, pointing towards Jim Bob. Jim Bob looked her directly in the eyes.

"Let me die with dignity," he said. "Make it quick."

Elysia paused, pretending to think his request over. Finally, she spoke, "No. You don't deserve a quick death."

The shadows fully engulfed Jim Bob, and he started to scream.

"You're dead!" Jim Bob yelled, seemingly to no one. "No! Not you, too! You died!"

Elysia knew what he was seeing. His worst nightmares. This was a skill that she had picked up years ago, one that Malvina had taught her, and Elysia had adapted to fit with her own set of abilities. Right now, Jim Bob was seeing illusions caused by his own mind. His deepest fears and regrets come to life to torment him.

Elysia stood and watched him. His eyes darted around, and he kept talking to phantoms only he could see. Eventually, blood started running from his ears, and he slumped over, dead. Elysia looked at Jim Bob's body impassively. He was dead, for sure. She turned and walked over to his lackeys, still held by tentacles of shadow and hidden in darkness only she could see through.

"Still alive?" she called out to the remaining two. She heard gasps of surprise in response. They had thought that Jim Bob could defeat her.

"How?" one of them asked. "How did you best our leader?"

"Simple," Elysia responded. "I was better than him. He was weak, and I was strong."

This was something that she had been taught her entire life. Weakness was punished in the Winter Court, and the stronger you were, the safer you were. "In this world, it's kill or be killed," her parents used to tell her.

Elysia commanded her shadows to squeeze. Strangled chokes came from the two humans.

"Please…" the other said, "Mercy…"

"Like you showed my father mercy?" Elysia said coldly. "I don't think so."

She let their bodies drop to the ground. Elysia dismissed all her shadows, and the camp reappeared, the light of dawn becoming visible once more.

Alone in a strange realm, surrounded by the bodies of her enemies, Elysia sat down on the ground and started to cry.

CHAPTER FOUR

Elysia didn't know how long she sat there, crying. Hours, minutes, she didn't care. She just sat there and mourned the death of her father. Eventually, she stood up and dried her tears.

She decided to look over the bodies. None of Jim Bob's comrades had anything interesting, just the basic traveling supplies, their greatswords, and the holy symbols of whatever god they worshiped. On the other hand, Jim Bob and his basic supplies had what looked to be a broken sending stone. Sending stones were used to communicate over long distances and must have been how Jim Bob communicated with the person who hired him. He must have destroyed it after they had finished communicating.

Seeing the stone made Elysia remember something. Malvina had given her and Wilfred a sending stone before they had left. The only problem was that Wilfred had been carrying it.

Elysia felt her eyes tear up when she thought about her father. Now that the humans were dead, nothing was distracting her from her grief. She pushed her feelings away. She had to move on.

What could she do in the meantime? She had no way of contacting her family. Could she hope Malvina would come looking for her if she waited long enough? They had been supposed to contact her when they arrived at Stonewood, and that was almost two days ago. And what should she do with the bodies? Did she just leave them to be discovered by some random traveler?

Eventually, Elysia decided to try to find her way back to the original spot where the portal had opened. She left the bodies where they were. They didn't deserve to be buried, and there was nothing at the site that could connect their deaths to her other than maybe some residual magic left in the area.

Nothing bothered Elysia as she walked through the forest. She saw some of those strange grey squirrels, but they minded their own business, and she encountered no sapient beings. After a while, Elysia realized she was lost. She had never really been in the wilderness before, other than exploring the forest around her house when she was a child. Being part of a noble family, she hadn't ever needed to know survival skills, and her magic was more useful in combat than in the middle of the woods.

After seeing the same tree seven times in a row, Elysia stopped walking. She realized that if Malvina would come and find her, it would be better for her to stay in one place.

Elysia sat down next to a tree and waited. She decided that she hated the human realm, hated humans, and really disliked traveling. By the time it was almost night, Elysia was beginning to think about finding a different place to sleep. She was not worried about getting attacked by an animal or person; she could handle herself in a fight, but the tree was a rather uncomfortable place to sleep. She got up and started walking around somewhat aimlessly.

After a minute, she heard a noise behind her. Summoning her Shadow Blade, Elysia whirled around to see what it was. Behind her, she saw her sister, Malvina.

"Malvina?" Elysia said, "You came to find me?"

Malvina looked at her with a sad expression. "What happened, Elysia?" she asked. "Where is Father? We were supposed to hear from you two days ago. Mother was concerned that something had happened and sent me to check on you."

Elysia dismissed her blade and hugged Malvina tightly. Malvina hugged her back. After a minute, she pulled away.

"It's okay, Elysia," she said, brushing Elysia's tears away. Elysia hadn't even realized that she had started crying. "Tell me what happened," Malvina said.

Elysia took a deep breath. "After Father and I arrived, we tried to use the house figure Mother gave us, but nothing happened. There was an antimagic circle. They knew we were coming beforehand somehow and had set the circle up. Then…" she trailed off.

Malvina waited for her to finish.

"Then the humans came. They were some kind of paladins, I think. They captured me and put me in iron manacles. They….killed Father. They put a wooden stake through his heart, and when we got to their camp, they burned him."

Malvina stayed silent, but her expression grew more horrified by the second.

Elysia continued, "Malvina, I think they were hired by someone. They wouldn't tell me who, but I know it was someone who knows our family."

Malvina nodded, "How did you escape with the iron?"

Elysia hesitated. Should she tell her sister? She trusted her, but… Elysia shooed those thoughts away. If she couldn't trust Malvina, there was no one she could trust. Besides, she wanted to know how she had done it, and Malvina knew more about magic than anyone else Elysia knew.

"I don't know," she said honestly. "I tried to go invisible, and it worked. It still hurt to use my magic through the iron, and it was harder to do, but I still did it."

Malvina thought for a moment. "I think it might be because you're only half Fey," she said. "But interestingly, I don't think I can do that, and Zia can't either. How did you get away from the humans?"

Elysia looked her in the eyes. "I killed them all," she said. "I used the illusion you taught me.

Malvina looked sad. "I hoped you would never have to use it," Malvina said. "I'm sorry you had to do that."

"I'm not," Elysia said.

Malvina hesitated for a moment. "Let's get you back home," she said.

Malvina summoned her demon bone staff and grabbed Elysia's hand as they disappeared.

CHAPTER FIVE

Elysia and Malvina appeared standing in the middle of the forest surrounding their home. Elysia had never been so happy to see the big stone house in the middle of the woods. It wasn't snowing anymore, and footlong icicles had grown on the house and trees. The icicles were glowing a soft blue. Her family lived near the heart of the Unseelie Court, where it was always winter. Elysia and Malvina walked over to the house and stepped inside. Inside, Sylvena and Zia were sitting in the living room. Sylvena immediately sat up and rushed over to Elysia.

"Elysia! Are you okay?" Sylvena said. "What happened?"

"I'm fine, Mother," Elysia said.

Malvina told Sylvena, "Mother, I need to talk to you. Elysia, Zia, go upstairs."

Elysia and Zia knew better than to argue. As they walked upstairs, Elysia heard Malvina speaking to their mother in hushed tones.

"What happened, Elysia?" Zia asked excitedly. "Where's Father?"

"I don't want to talk about it," Elysia said. "Malvina will tell you."

"I don't want to hear it from Malvina. I want to hear from you. What happened?"

Elysia was sick of people asking, "What happened?"

"Leave me alone, Ziara," she said, using Zia's full name, which she knew she hated. "I'm tired, I need a change of clothes, I feel like I need to sleep for three days, and I'm sick of your questions."

Zia glared. "Fine. If you don't tell me, I will try to hear what Mother and Malvina are discussing."

She turned away, leaving Elysia at the entrance to her room. Elysia walked inside. The first thing she did was collapse on her bed, falling asleep within minutes.

When Elysia woke up, she changed into a dark purple dress with a long skirt and long sleeves and brushed and braided her hair. She opened her door and found Zia standing outside, her arms crossed and with a scowl on her face.

Elysia sighed. "What is it now, Zia?"

"Father is dead," Zia said softly. "And you didn't tell me."

Elysia now noticed that Zia had clearly been crying. "I'm sorry, Zia… I just…" Elysia trailed off. "I couldn't talk about it," she finished. "It was better that you heard from Malvina anyway."

Zia stood silently for a moment before walking away. She only got a few feet away before she started crying again. She picked up her pace and disappeared behind a corner.

Elysia didn't follow her. She and Zia had never been very close, even though they were only ten years apart. It was unusual for the Fey to have children so close in age; most siblings were centuries apart. Elysia and Zia had grown up together and trained together, and they were both very competitive. Elysia had also been more skilled than Zia in fighting, and she suspected Zia had always resented her for that.

In a society where weakness was ignored or punished, Elysia had always strived to be the best. Elysia had always gotten along better with Malvina, who had always spent time helping to train her in her magic.

Elysia stood in the doorway to her room. She didn't want to go and face her mother and Malvina. She knew that both of them would be worried about her. They would be concerned, ask her questions, and pretend everything was fine. She didn't need them watching her and taking care of her.

She thought about Zia and the sad, betrayed look on her face. Seeing her younger sister so upset made her start to think about when Wilfred had died. Elysia ignored those emotions. She would be fine; she just needed time to avoid thinking about that day. Zia was the one they should be paying attention to, not her.

Elysia turned around and started walking back into her room. Maybe she could just hide out and take a nap. She knew that was foolish, but she was tired and didn't want to face her family.

When she turned around, however, he saw her mother sitting on her bed. Elysia sighed. Even though Sylvena didn't use advanced teleportation like Malvina, she was perfectly capable of appearing anywhere within a short distance.

"How are you doing, Elysia?" Her mother asked. "Malvina told me what happened, so I know you've had a rough couple of days."

"I'll be fine," Elysia replied. It was true. She would be fine. Eventually. She sat down on her bed next to her mother.

"Are you sure?" Sylvena said.

"I should be asking you that," Elysia responded. Her parents had been together for over three hundred years, and she knew her mother wasn't as composed as she seemed.

Sylvena evaded the question, "Your father was a great person, and I'm sure we will all cherish the time that we had with him, however short it was."

Elysia didn't push it. She knew her mother had to be grieving. She probably just didn't want to upset her.

Elysia changed the topic. "Mother, did Malvina tell you what I thought of?"

"What do you mean?" Syvena said.

"I think that the entire event was planned. It's no coincidence that those humans were there. They knew who we were, and they tried to kidnap me for whoever hired them. I also think this mysterious benefactor must have been a Fey or someone else who might have a vendetta against our family. Do you think it could be someone from the Seelie Court?"

Historically, the summer and winter Fey did not get along, and even if specific members forged temporary alliances, their Queens had always been rivals.

Sylvena smiled at her. "You might be reading too much into this, Elysia. It could have just been the wrong place at the wrong time. Why don't you get some rest?"

Elysia frowned. Her mother wasn't telling her something. All of the Fey, including Elysia and her mother, couldn't tell direct lies, and there was something strange about the way Sylvena phrased her words.

"Okay…" Elysia said unconvincingly. "It could just be nothing…"

Her mother left, closing the door behind her. *What is going on?* Elysia thought.

INTERLUDE
– TEN YEARS AGO

Zia brought up her sword to block her sister's blade. Elysia quickly moved to the side, lashing out at Zia again. Zia moved out of the way and tried to locate her sister. Had she gone to the other side of the courtyard? She couldn't see Elysia anywhere. All of a sudden, she felt someone kick her in the back. Zia stumbled, tripping in the sand. When she regained her balance, she saw Elysia standing before her. Her blade pointed at Zia.

"Looks like I won again," Elysia said after she had dismissed her blade.

"You cheated!" Zia said, indignant.

She and Elysia had been training in the courtyard behind their house. Standing behind them on the courtyard's edge was Malvina, who had been observing them.

"I did what I needed to win," Elysia said.

"Good job, but next time, don't cheat," Malvina responded.

Zia rolled her eyes. She would have been able to win, but of course, Elysia had used her magic. It was *supposed* to be a weapons-only duel. Zia looked at the sword in her hand. It was just a normal weapon made of metal. Zia couldn't make a weapon with her magic yet, unlike Elysia, who could create a blade of shadows.

Zia tried to summon something small, like a knife. After a minute of concentration, a small knife made of crystalized ice appeared in her hand. As soon as it appeared, however, it shattered into shards of ice that melted as soon as they touched the ground. She had inherited ice magic from her great-grandmother. Even though her grandmother was a powerful Archfey, Zia sometimes felt like the skills may have skipped a generation.

Elysia saw the ice fall to the ground and walked over to Zia. "Don't worry, Zia," Elysia said. "You'll get it eventually. It took me years to learn how to summon my blade. Besides, you don't even technically need a weapon. Look at Malvina—she doesn't use a sword."

"I know," Zia replied, "but I still want to learn how. If you can do it, then so can I."

Zia didn't want to just rely on magic. She wanted to use a blade and magic, like Elysia did. Besides, she couldn't stand sitting in a library, reading books all day like Malvina did. Zia sighed and let the metal sword drop to the ground.

Elysia bid goodbye to Zia and ran over to the door of the house, no doubt excited to tell their parents about her accomplishment. Zia sighed and sat down in a chair next to Malvina. She looked over at the book that Malvina had in her hands. The book was thick and bound in red leather.

"What are you reading, Malvina?" Zia asked.

"I'm writing," Malvina responded absentmindedly.

"Well, what are you writing?" Zia said, annoyed. Malvina tended to get lost in her research and probably hadn't even been watching Zia and Elysia's duel the entire time.

Malvina closed her book. "I'm writing about demons," she responded.

Zia immediately looked to the staff, leaning on the wall next to Malvina. It was made from the bone of a demon that had killed many of Malvina's friends. Zia didn't know anything more than that it had happened before she and

Elysia were born. She also didn't know anything about the mysterious grey orb attached to the top of the staff. Malvina had never told them anything about it, and sometimes Zia and Elysia theorized about what it could be. Whenever they told Malvina their theories, she just shook her head and told them they didn't need to know.

"Is it about demons you have encountered?" Zia asked. She was always interested to hear more about her older sister's life.

"Yes, it is." Malvina said, smiling. "You can read it when you're older."

"I'm old enough to read it now," Zia said. She was almost thirty-one, and Malvina still treated her like she was a child.

"I know you are," Malvina said sadly, "but there are still some things you don't need to know."

Then she closed the book and walked away, leaving Zia with more questions than answers.

CHAPTER SIX

The following morning, Elysia sat at the dining room table, eating a croissant. She loved croissants and was on her third one of the morning. It was peaceful in the house as the rest of her family was out in the courtyard enjoying the day.

The goblin housekeeper, Krigs, walked out of the kitchen holding a pot of tea. Krigs was about three feet tall, had a big head with big ears, and always wore a suit. He looked about mid-fifties. Krigs had been in the family's employ for about a hundred years and lived in a small apartment attached to the kitchen. He also made excellent croissants.

Krigs set the pot of tea on the table next to Elysia. After pouring them both a cup of tea, he sat down and looked over at the piece of paper in front of her.

"Might I inquire what you are doing, Miss Elysia?" Krigs asked. Even though Elysia had known him her entire life, he still formally addressed her and everyone in the household. Elysia set down her croissant, picking up the paper.

"I'm trying to figure something out," Elysia said.

The paper she was holding was covered in writing, with arrows drawn to connect certain sections. Unlike Zia, Elysia enjoyed writing and reading and had even read some of Malvina's books, although she hadn't found them particularly interesting.

Krigs nodded sagely. "And what is it you are trying to understand?" he asked, patient as always.

"Who *really* killed my father?" Elysia said. "I can't figure it out. Why would a bunch of humans want to be with our family? More importantly, who hired them? My mother is acting strange about the whole event, and I think she isn't telling me something. I just don't understand."

She sighed and set down the paper, slumping in her chair. Krigs reached over, patted her on the shoulder, and handed her a cup of tea.

"I'm sure you'll figure something out," Krigs said.

Then he got up and left to go back to the kitchen. Elysia sat for another minute, staring at her notes. When no more ideas came to mind, she put her notes in her pocket, grabbed her cup of tea, and went outside to see what her family was doing.

When she stepped outside, she saw Malvina and Zia sitting at a table outside. Malvina was reading a book, and Zia was tapping her fingers on the table, looking bored. Elysia was happy to be home. It was comforting to have some semblance of normalcy, even with the giant void left by Wilfred's death. She even saw a squirrel made of blue fire with black voids for eyes hop from one tree to another outside the courtyard. It was nice to see some normal wildlife finally.

"Where's Mother?" Elysia asked, sitting down next to her sisters.

"I don't know," Zia said. "She just left and said she'd return soon. Said we shouldn't follow her."

Elysia shrugged. Their mother did this occasionally, sometimes disappearing for hours before returning and not speaking of where she had been.

Elysia looked to Malvina. "Can I talk with you about something, Malvina?" she asked, shooting a glance at Zia.

"I'm not leaving," Zia said. "If you want to talk to Malvina about something, you can talk to me as well."

"Well, it's not that I don't think you need to know. I just wanted to speak with Malvina first," Elysia said, annoyed.

Her little sister wanted to be involved in everything, even if people didn't want her to be. Zia crossed her arms and gave Elysia a defiant look. She clearly wasn't going to leave. Elysia ignored her. If she wanted to stay and listen, she could.

Elysia spoke to Malvina. "I need your opinion on this," she said, bringing the piece of paper out of the pocket of her dress.

Malvina set down her book and took the piece of paper from Elysia. She was silent for a few moments before she spoke. "I don't know, Elysia."

"What is it?" Zia asked.

"I'm trying to figure out who's behind Father's death," Elysia said.

"You were trying to keep this from me?" Zia asked. "I didn't even know you thought someone had orchestrated it! Besides, I could help you find out who did it!"

Elysia was surprised. She hadn't expected Zia to be so angry.

"I wasn't trying to keep anything from you, Ziara," Elysia said.

"You never tell me anything," Zia said. "You wouldn't even talk to me after Father was killed. And *don't* call me that."

"Well, maybe I didn't feel like reliving the event so that you could get firsthand information."

"This whole situation is your fault in the first place, Elysia. You got to go to the human realm, and now that Father's gone, I can't go with him when it's my birthday."

"So, according to you, it's my fault that Father is dead and I was kidnapped?"

Elysia got up out of her chair, angry with her sister now. Zia also got up, pointing an accusatory finger at Elysia.

"Yes! Father would still be alive if you had never wanted to go on that stupid trip. You always get what you want just because you're the favourite."

"You don't know what you're talking about, Zia. None of this is my fault any more than it is yours. We didn't know that the humans would be there."

"You don't understand, Elysia," Zia said with tears in her eyes. "You ruined everything. It's your fault that Father is dead. And I will never forgive you."

"It's *not* my fault!" Elysia said. "What are you even talking about?"

"Stop fighting," Malvina said, finally having enough of her sister's argument.

Zia ignored her. "You don't realize how your decisions affect other people, Elysia. Life is so easy for you."

"No, It's not, Zia," Elysia said. She was quite angry now. "Do you think it was easy for me to watch Father die? Were you there, Zia? Did you see them drive a wooden stake through his heart? Do you think it's easy to stand here and listen to you blame me for your difficulties? No, Zia, I don't think my life is particularly easy at all right now."

Elysia also had tears in her eyes now. She looked around the courtyard and realized all the shadows were moving, slowly closing in on Zia.

Malvina spoke again, sitting up and stepping between Zia and Elysia, "Elysia, stop it. Go take a walk and cool off. Zia, I'm going to have a word with you right now."

Malvina walked over to Zia, grabbed her arm, and marched her out of the room and into the house. Zia didn't bother struggling. With Malvina being so much older than Elysia and Zia, she was almost like another parent, and they knew when to listen to her.

Zia turned her head to watch Elysia as Malvina dragged her into the house. The courtyard was still covered in shadows. It was ironic, Zia thought, that Elysia insisted that she wasn't special, but she didn't even seem to notice when she used immense amounts of magic. Zia could never accomplish something on that scale.

Her thoughts were interrupted when Malvina shut the door loudly. She turned and spoke to Zia.

"Zia, what do you think you're doing?" Malvina said. "Do you realize that what you say affects other people?"

Zia looked around. She realized that they were in Malvina's room in the house. Even though Malvina rarely stayed home, she still had a place to stay when she returned from her adventures.

"I think that—" Zia began, but she was cut off when Malvina spoke again.

"No, Zia, this isn't the part where you talk. This is the part where you *listen*. It wasn't right of you to speak to Elysia that way. You don't understand what she's been through. Have you ever seen a parent or a close companion get murdered right in front of your eyes? I have. Elysia has."

Zia realized that Malvina must be referring to her first adventuring group. She didn't know the specifics, but apparently, they had all been killed, and Malvina had been the only survivor.

"Do you think that you're the only one who has been affected by Father's death?" Malvina continued. "It's been hard for all of us. I'm convinced that Mother has fallen into depression, but she's trying to hide it from us. Elysia seems hell-bent on revenge, and I'm barely managing to keep this family from falling apart." She paused and took a deep breath. "I expect you to apologize to Elysia. And if you're really so jealous of her, then just improve. It's really not that difficult."

"I…" Zia trailed off.

She was torn between two points of view. To some extent, she understood what Malvina was telling her. But at the same time, she felt like none of them understood *her*. If Malvina said they were *all* struggling, why did she seem so focused on Elysia?

"You don't understand, do you?" Zia finally said. "That's what I've been trying to do my entire life. It's not as easy for me as it is for you or Elysia. All I've heard my whole life is, 'You just need to try harder, Zia,' or 'It's not your fault that Elysia is more talented. You just need to do better.' Well, I'm tired of trying harder and being told that I just need to do better. It seems that my best will never be enough."

Malvina sighed. "Zia..." she said, "I can't handle this right now. If you're going to be petulant and childish, then I don't have time for it. I'm going to wait for Elysia to come back. Stay here, and think about what you're going to say to her. I'll come and get you when she's about to return."

"I know you're angry with me," Zia said as Malvina walked out of the room, "and I will apologize to Elyisa, but I stand by what I said."

Malvina stopped in the doorway and turned to look at Zia. "I'm not angry, Zia," she said. "I'm just disappointed."

Then Malvina left, closing the door behind her. Zia stood for a moment and then immediately tried to leave. The door didn't open. Had her sister really locked her in here?

Zia sighed and kicked the door halfheartedly. There wasn't much she could do to try and get out. For all she knew, Malvina had cursed the door to explode if anyone tried to open it. Zia sat in a chair next to a small table with an open book.

She looked around Malvina's room. It looked less like a bedroom and more like a researcher's study. There were notes covering the walls, written in Malvina's handwriting but in a language that Zia didn't know. There were books everywhere. On shelves, on the floor, and stacked up on the windowsill.

As Zia looked around the room, something caught her eye. A thin cabinet in the corner of the room. She walked over and investigated it. Inside was the strangest collection of objects. A shrunken head, a small teacup stained with blood, and other oddities. Zia began to walk away, and the shrunken head slowly turned to watch her. She really didn't want to know where Malvina had gotten the head.

Zia returned to the chair she had been sitting in. She looked at the book on the table. It was thick, with a red leather cover. Something about it was familiar. She picked it up and looked at the open page. It was a chapter about the dangers of summoning devils. Boring. Zia began looking through the pile of scattered objects on the table. Zia could leave it alone. Or she could make her sister's life just a little more difficult.

Zia picked up the items one by one. A strange glowing crystal? Easily replaced. A shell that sparked in the shadows, not the light? Too mundane. She finally picked up a small vial of blood hanging from a leather cord. Hmm…, not easily replaced, but clearly not important enough to keep separate from a scattered pile. She pocketed it and began reading the strange book.

About an hour later, Zia heard someone coming up the stairs. She quickly put the book down. Malvian opened the door a second later.

"Follow me, Zia," she said. "Elysia's back."

Zia walked out, shooting one last glance back at the book. She didn't mind having to confront Elysia. After all, she now had a *plan*.

CHAPTER SEVEN

When Malvina and Zia were gone, Elysia quickly walked to the other side of the courtyard and through the side door. She didn't even know where she was going. She just walked in a random direction, trudging through the snow. Snow had started falling, and the forest was very quiet. The trees looked like tall, scraggly skeletons, casting ominous shadows. Some of the trees *were* actual skeletons, the remains of creatures that had died long ago, turned into trees of bone. It may have been a sunny day, but the deeper she went into the woods, the less light there was. Soon, Elysia couldn't even see any light, and the entire forest was dark as night. The dark didn't impede her ability to see, so she continued walking.

Elysia couldn't believe some of the things that Zia had said. She didn't know how much Elysia had struggled through the past few days. Elysia had been trying not to focus on the day that her father had died, but now that was all that she could think about. Maybe it *was* her fault. She could have tried to fight the humans off. She still didn't know how they had known that they would be there.

She guessed that whoever had hired them had found out somehow and told them. She probably should have kept one of the humans alive and interrogated them, even though they probably wouldn't have talked. Elysia looked around at the forest.

Suddenly, it reminded her of the forest in the human realm. Even though the two forests were extremely different, they seemed similar to her at that moment. She thought about how much she despised Jim Bob. She didn't regret what had happened to him. He had deserved it. She sat down next to one of the trees, trying to forget what had happened that day.

After sitting in the middle of the woods for quite some time, Elysia began to think that maybe she should go home. The wilds of the Winter Court really weren't the safest place to be, even in the middle of the day, and Malvina was probably worried about her. She looked around and saw a flock of small birds that were made of twigs. They started chirping at her, clearly annoyed at her presence. Elysia hastily got up and started walking back home, brushing snow off her clothes. She wasn't sure what species of twig birds they were, and it was more likely they were dangerous than not.

After walking for a minute or two, Elysia realized she didn't recognize this part of the forest. She should probably learn how to navigate the wilderness, as she had found herself getting lost quite often lately. She decided to just walk in the vague direction of her house. She would find it eventually.

Elysia heard a scuffling noise and shouting from behind a tree along the way. She quickly made the shadows surround her, obscuring her from sight. She quietly crept closer to the shouting. She peeked around a tree. She saw a group of three short creatures clustered around a box. One was a Redcap, a three-foot-tall gnome-like creature with a red hat carrying a sickle. Redcaps were nasty little creatures, always causing violence and chaos. They got their name from the hats they wore, which they dipped in the blood of their victims. They were attracted to the aftermath of large battles. Along with the Redcap were two tiny Sprites, a type of small Faerie. Both the sprites carried tiny longbows.

Elysia couldn't hear what they were saying, so she quietly walked closer. Now that she was closer, she saw that the box they were so focused on was actually a small cage. Inside was a Displacer Beast kitten. Displacer Beasts were large, pony-sized cats with six legs and two tentacles coming out of their backs. They used the tentacles to project an illusion of themselves to confuse their prey. Displacer Beasts were native to the Unseelie Court, and while they were mainly wild, they were sometimes kept as guards or familiars.

"Keep the cat quiet," the Redcap said to the Sprites. "Let's get out of here."

"You got it," one of the Sprites said.

It pulled out a tiny arrow and dipped it in a jar. Probably a tranquilizer or sleeping potion. The other Sprite flew around in circles.

"We're going to make so much money!" it said.

They would probably sell it on the Black Market, or someone had hired them to find the kitten. Elysia watched as the first Sprite drew back its bow, aiming at the kitten. The kitten meowed and backed away.

Elysia made a split-second decision. She wasn't going to let them sell this poor little Displacer Beast. Besides, this was her family's part of the forest, and these creatures needed to be taught not to cross them. Elysia stepped out from behind the tree, dispersing her invisibility.

"Stop," she said. The entire group froze. The Redcap moved in front of the cage, trying to block the kitten from view.

"Oh… um… hello," the Redcap said.

"What are you doing with that Displacer Beast?" Elysia asked. "Not to mention, what are you doing in this forest? Who let you come here?"

"What are you doing here?" the Redcap countered. "Were you following us? Who are you?"

It seemed like this little group didn't want anyone to find out what they were doing.

"My name is Elysia Moonwatcher," she said. "And I don't think that my family will be very pleased to know what you're doing in our forest. Although, I don't think I need to mention what you were doing… for a small favour."

The Redcap motioned over to the two Sprites, and they huddled around his head, whispering. After a moment of deliberation, the Redcap turned toward Elysia again.

"What do you want?" he asked.

Elysia grinned, "I won't mention that you were here in exchange for the Displacer Beast."

The Redcap responded immediately, "No way."

Elysia directed the shadows to move closer to the Redcap and his companions, slowly closing in on them. "It would be a shame if you didn't return from your perilous mission," Elysia said. "You invaded my family's land without our permission. I'm well within my rights to punish you as I see fit."

She paused for a moment. "Or I could make it look like an accident. Displacer Beasts are very dangerous creatures, after all."

The Redcap looked around in panic. "Fine," he said, "take the cat."

He quickly rushed away from Elysia, his companions flying after him. Elysia watched them scramble away. They wouldn't be coming back anytime soon. She was surprised that the Redcap hadn't stayed and tried to fight. Apparently, he knew when he was outclassed. Anyway, this encounter was a good way to spread her reputation and show that her family wasn't to be messed with.

Elysia walked over to the cage that held the Displacer Beast kitten. She unlatched the cage and stepped back. The kitten didn't walk out at first, but eventually, it cautiously stepped out. It sat on the ground in front of Elysia. It cocked its head to one side and swished its tail back and forth.

Displacer Beasts were intelligent, and this kitten didn't seem afraid of her.

"Hello," Elysia said. "My name is Elysia."

The cat just stared at her. Elysia wasn't a druid and didn't have a way of communicating with animals. Displacer Beasts were intelligent and understood speech, but they didn't speak.

"What happened to your family?" Elysia asked.

The kitten meowed mournfully in response. That could have meant anything from that they had died to the kitten missing them to the kitten not knowing.

Elysia sighed. "I don't know what you mean," she said, "but I'm going to go back to my home. You can follow me if you want."

She started walking in the direction she thought her house was. Surprisingly, the kitten followed her, its six legs letting it keep up easily.

After walking for half an hour, Elysia spotted the large stone building in the distance. She and the cat walked up to the door, which she opened, letting the kitten walk in first. Elysia went over to the kitchen and spotted Krigs inside, preparing some kind of food.

"Krigs," Elysia called, "we have a guest. Could you please prepare something for them?"

Krigs stepped away from the counter and looked at the Displacer Beast. "Of course!" he said.

Krigs gestured for the cat to come to the kitchen. "Please tell me what you would like me to prepare."

The kitten leaped up on the counter and dragged a piece of raw bacon onto the floor. One of the kittens' tentacles hit a jar of flour on its way down, and flour spilled over the counter. Krigs sighed and began cleaning up the mess.

Elysia laughed and watched the kitten finish its bacon. When it was finished, Elysia walked into the main room, the kitten following her. She saw Zia and Malvina sitting on a couch. They both looked at her, then at the Displacer Beast.

"Where did you find a *Displacer Beast?*" Zia asked when she saw Elysia. "You leave for an hour and then come back with a cat."

Malvina sighed. "I think you mean to say something else, Zia."

Zia glared at her. She got up and approached Elysia, "I'm sorry, Elysia. I shouldn't have yelled at you earlier."

She shot a glare at Elysia before turning back to Malvina. Elysia thought about what she had said. She hadn't said that she regretted anything she had said, only that she shouldn't have yelled at her. Zia had probably only said that to please Malvina.

Very clever, Zia, Elysia thought. Zia had gotten better at avoiding saying what she didn't want to without lying. Elysia had always found it easy to misdirect and avoid questions with non-answers. It seemed like Zia was finally catching up. She could have called Zia out for not apologizing directly, but she was too tired to start another argument.

"I appreciate that, Zia, and I hope nothing like that happens again."

Zia said nothing, turning to the kitten instead. It seemed like neither of them wanted to argue in front of Malvina. Elysia sat down on the floor next to the kitten. The little Displacer Beast hopped up into her lap and started purring.

"I think it likes you, Elysia," Malvina said, sitting next to the cat as well.

A few minutes later, Sylvena walked through the door. She looked at her daughters, all sitting at the table with a Displacer Beast kitten. She looked stunned for a moment.

"I'm not even going to ask," Sylvena said. "At least not until I've had coffee."

She walked into the kitchen. After she came out, holding a large mug of coffee, she spoke. "All right, which one of you brought this home?" Sylvena asked, looking accusingly at her daughters.

"I found it," Elysia said. "Please don't make me get rid of it. I don't think it has a family."

Sylvena sighed, "Where did you find it, Elysia?"

"I was taking a walk," Elysia shot an annoyed glance at Zia, "and I found a Redcap and some Sprites. They had captured this poor little baby, and I convinced them to give it to me."

She paused. "Do you think you can talk to it? I'm not very good at speaking to animals."

Sylvena considered Elysia's request for a moment. "I'll talk to it, but if it has a home, it can't stay."

"Okay," Elysia said.

She handed the cat to her mother. Sylvena set the cat on the table to get closer to eye level. Nothing visible happened, but the little cat tilted its head to the side. Sylvena was speaking with it telepathically.

After a minute of silence, Sylvena spoke to Elysia. "She says her name is Nyx. She doesn't know what happened to her parents, only that they didn't return one day. She didn't have any other littermates. A day after her parents didn't return, the Redcap took her from her cave. She said that she wants to stay with Elysia."

Elysia spoke to the cat, "Hello, Nyx. I'm sorry about your parents. I lost my father recently as well. You can definitely stay if you want to."

Sylvena turned back to the cat. "She said that she would like that," Sylvena said.

Elysia grinned and picked the cat up off the table. "I'm so excited!" she said. "I think we're going to be great friends."

She looked at Sylvena, "Could you teach me the spell to talk with Nyx?"

Sylvena smiled, "Of course."

Elysia started to get up, but Sylvena held up a finger.

"Not right now," she said, "since all of you are here, I have something to share with you."

Elysia and her sisters glanced at each other. If their mother was talking to all of them together, it must be something important.

"While I was gone," Sylvena said, "I was speaking to your great-grandmother. She wants to visit."

That surprised Elysia. Their great-grandmother was a powerful Archfey, a close ally of the Winter Queen. She rarely visited her descendants, so her coming now was unexpected.

"Why is she coming now?" Elysia asked.

"You'll find out when she gets here," Sylvena said.

"When is she coming?" Zia asked. "I want to meet her. Is she nice?" Despite being over forty years old, Zia had never met their great-grandmother.

"Soon," Sylvena said. "And she's an Archfey from the Winter Court. I wouldn't make her angry. No one gets by in society by being nice."

She turned to Zia. "Why don't you help Krigs make some scones and tea before she comes?"

Zia sighed, petted Nyx one more time, and got up, muttering about how they just wanted to get rid of her for a minute and how Sylvena knew she hated baking.

Once she was gone, Sylvena told Nyx, "If you're going to stay with us, I need you to promise you won't reveal any of our secrets. In turn, you will be treated as a member of the family."

Nyx tilted her head to the side and meowed affirmingly. This seemed to be good enough for Sylvena, as she then turned her attention to Malvina and Elysia.

"Your grandmother has something planned," Sylvena said. "I don't know exactly what, but I have an idea. Be prepared for her to ask you to do something."

She gave both of them a stern look and then left the room. Malvina and Elysia looked at each other with confusion on their faces.

CHAPTER EIGHT

Sylvena, Malvina, Elysia, and Zia were all seated in their living room, waiting for their grandmother to arrive. Nyx was sleeping upstairs in Elysia's room. Elysia didn't know much about baby Displacer Beasts, but apparently, they slept a *lot*.

Krigs walked out of the kitchen holding a tray of tea and scones. He set the tray down on a small table nearby, next to a stack of books.

"Tea and scones," he said.

"Those look delicious, Krigs," Sylvena said. Zia immediately reached for one of the scones.

"Zia!" Elysia said, "wait for our guest to arrive. You need to remember your manners."

Zia glared at her, "I helped make these scones," she muttered, but she put the scone back despite her protesting.

"If you need anything else, please inform me," Krigs said. He bowed and walked back to the kitchen.

They all sat in silence for a few minutes. Zia was about to speak when their grandmother appeared in the middle of the room.

Illiyith, the matriarch of House Moonwatcher, didn't look like an average grandmother. She looked about mid to late twenties and was tall, with icy blue skin and bright silver hair and eyes. She was wearing a black dress and carrying a staff made of ice crystals in one hand. Her gaze swept over her descendants.

"Hello, children," she said. Her voice had a commanding presence.

"Grandmother," they all echoed. Illiyith sat down on a chair across from Elysia.

"I know that my visit must be unexpected," Illiyith said, "especially with all the sorrow your family has endured in the last few days."

She looked at Elysia. "I do have a good reason for coming, I assure you."

Elysia was nervous. Why was her grandmother looking at her specifically? Was she disappointed in her?

Illiyith continued, "I have come to wish my granddaughter a happy birthday."

Elysia was stunned. Her grandmother had come for her birthday, and she barely knew her. Elysia wanted to speak, but she knew better than to interrupt her grandmother.

Illiyith smiled. "I've been watching you, and your actions in the past days have impressed me. I would like to speak to you privately now."

She glanced at the others. Sylvena, not wanting to displease Illiyith, quickly ushered her other children upstairs. Elysia was surprised that she had told the rest of her family to leave so quickly. Apparently, she liked to get to the point of things and not spend time on pleasantries.

Once they were alone, Illiyith looked Elysia directly in the eye. "I know who killed your father," she said.

"What?" Elysia said, stunned.

"I know who hired those humans that attacked you. I don't want to act directly, so I need you to act for me. Next week, there is a party in a secret location. All of this person's potential allies will be there. I have an invitation so that you will be granted entry. Just read the invitation aloud, and it will transport you to the location. Gather as much information as you can, then report back to me. Your mother doesn't want you to get caught up in what's going on, but I'm afraid it might be too late."

"I don't mean to be rude," Elysia said, "but why not Malvina? She's more powerful than I am and has more experience."

Illiyith gave her an unnerving smile and handed her a piece of paper. "Your sister isn't what I need for this mission. I don't think I need to tell you this is a test. Don't tell your sisters where you are going. I have big plans for you, Elysia. Do not disappoint me."

Then she vanished, leaving Elysia alone at the table. Elysia looked at the piece of paper in her hands. It was an invitation to a gathering set to occur a week from now. The location wasn't written on the invitation. Elysia put it in her extradimensional storage space and called her family downstairs.

Zia spoke the moment she was downstairs. "Well, that was abrupt. She didn't even acknowledge me," she said sadly. "She only paid attention to Elysia."

"I told you that she was like that," Malvina said. "You must prove yourself before she'll pay you any attention."

Malvina then picked up a book from the table and began to read, ignoring her sister.

Zia sighed, "I'm still sad." She turned her attention to Elysia. "What did she talk to you about? I don't think she came just to wish you a happy birthday."

"I can't tell you, Zia. I do need to go somewhere soon, though."

"It's not fair," Zia complained, sitting on a couch and nibbling on a scone. "I meet my great-grandmother for the first time, and all she cares about is Elysia. Elysia gets a gift. Elysia gets a special quest."

"It's not my fault," Elysia said. "I don't even know why she likes me."

"Don't bicker," Sylvena chided them.

"Fine," Zia said, picking up another scone. She glared at Elysia as if the whole situation was somehow her fault.

"Elysia, how about we go up to the library?" Sylvena asked.

"Okay…" Elysia said. She started walking up the stairs, glancing back at her sisters.

The library took up the entire third floor of the house. Bookshelves of various subjects lined the walls, and there was a large table in the center of the room, with books scattered across its surface. Magical lanterns hung from the ceiling, giving off a warm glow. Elysia sat at the table, and her mother sat beside her.

"I was hoping she wouldn't ask you. I don't want you doing this, Elysia," Sylvena said. "It's too dangerous."

"Grandmother gave me this mission, Mother," Elysia said. "I need to know who killed Father."

"You need to stay safe," her mother argued. "I don't want you to get hurt."

"I'll be fine. Besides, grandmother wouldn't send me to do anything too dangerous, right? It's just gathering information."

They sat in silence. They both knew Illiyith wouldn't care how dangerous the situation was if it meant achieving her goals.

Finally, Sylvena said, "If you really think you need to do this, I won't stop you."

"You won't regret this, Mother," Elysia said, relieved. She would have had to sneak out if she hadn't let her go. "I won't be gone long. And please don't tell Malvina or Zia. Grandmother doesn't want them to know for some reason."

Sylvena nodded, and Elysia left the library, going downstairs to get some of the scones before Zia ate them all.

CHAPTER NINE

One week later, Elysia stood in her room, arguing with a cat. "I told you already, Nyx," she said. "You can't come with me."

Nyx looked up at her and let out a mournful meow. Ever since she had been staying with Elysia and her family, she had become very attached to Elysia and had some separation anxiety.

But I want to come, Elysia heard Nyx's voice in her mind. Sylvena had taught her the spell for speaking with animals, and she had been talking with Nyx quite often. Well, as often as Nyx wanted to speak with her. She still preferred meowing and other cat ways of communication.

I can be helpful, Nyx continued *I'm a fierce hunter! Remember the rat I killed a few days ago?*

Elysia did indeed remember the rat. She had been asleep, and Nyx had dropped the dead rat beside her—a very unpleasant way to wake up.

"Yes, you're very brave," Elysia said, "but I need to do this myself. You need to stay home and be very quiet."

Elysia didn't want Nyx meowing and waking up her sisters. Elysia had told her sisters that she was going to a party that only she had been invited to, which was true. She was going to a party. A party where her enemies could be. A party where the host was the person who had orchestrated her father's death.

She didn't know what kind of gathering it would be, so she had just worn a plain black dress with silver embroidery. She had chosen one with shorter sleeves and a slimmer skirt, just in case she had to fight her way out.

After giving Nyx a pat on the head, Elysia shut the door and carefully walked outside. It was dark outside, but it wasn't snowing anymore. Elysia pulled the invitation out of her storage space and read it aloud.

She was instantly transported to a different location. The teleportation had been fast, with little to no lag. Whoever made these invitations either had a lot of money or was very skilled in teleportation magic, like Malvina.

Elysia looked around. She was in the middle of a forest, very similar to the one she had just been in. She was still in the Winter Court, but there was less snowfall, and some of the trees still had leaves. Elysia realized that it wasn't snowing actual snow, but small triangular ice crystals. However, as soon as they hit the forest floor, they transformed into fluffy snow. The weather was more varied at the court's edges, so Elysia paid little attention.

About twenty yards in front of her was a massive tree, easily a hundred feet tall, with a trunk that must have been at least thirty feet in diameter. The bottom part of the trunk had grown into a cave shape, and windows were going up all the way to the branches. Light was coming from the cave and the windows, and she could see people inside.

Elysia thought about what she should do. She could just walk inside and start talking to people, but what if someone recognized her? Would that be an issue?

Another option was to go invisible, sneak inside, and try to listen in on what people were talking about. She might be able to get more information just by talking to people, but then again, they might talk more freely if they didn't know they were being listened to. She decided to sneak in, and if she didn't get anything useful, try talking to people.

Elysia made herself invisible. Her invisibility didn't work like most people's. Instead of going translucent, she was cloaked in shadow and blended in with the darkness. It worked less efficiently in the light but was extremely powerful and hard to detect in the shadow.

With her shadows around her, Elysia walked inside the giant tree. Inside was a large crowd of Fey, everything from high Fey like Elysia and her family to goblins to Faerie Dragons. Faerie dragons were small, intelligent Fey dragons with butterfly wings who liked to play tricks on people. Even as she thought this, Elysia saw a neon blue Faerie Dragon grab a drink off a table and pour it on someone's shoes before scampering away. Elysia had always found them annoying and endearing at the same time.

Elysia saw a staircase on one side of the tree, spiraling up inside the trunk. She didn't see anyone nearby and snuck up the staircase. At the top was a locked door with a small window in it. She peered through the window. All that she saw was more stairs. Probably a private residence. Did someone live inside the tree? It wasn't really that strange. Elysia had distant cousins in the Wyldfae who lived in a giant mushroom.

After checking out the stairs, Elysia tried listening in on some conversations. After about an hour of snooping, Elysia didn't find out anything that interesting. Everyone was just gossiping about meaningless things. This Fey's cousin had moved far away, this goblin finally had over two thousand individual human fingers, and someone's aunt was getting married.

Elysia decided that if she wanted to learn anything of real value, she needed to talk to people. She stepped outside the tree, checked that no one was nearby, and made herself visible again. She walked back inside, trying to appear nonchalant.

Elysia realized that she was nervous. All of the parties that she had been to in the past had been full of her family's political allies, and she had known most of the people there, and her family had been there with her. She steeled herself. This was important; she was going to find out who had killed her father, and she was going to make her grandmother proud.

A dark blue Faerie Dragon wearing a little bow tie flew up to her with a plate of snacks. "Would you like an appetizer, Miss?" the tiny dragon asked with a squeaky voice.

Elysia was going to decline, but the tiny dragon was just too adorable.

Elysia nodded and picked up a snack. It was a cheese sandwich in the shape of a star. After a moment of consideration, Elysia asked the Faerie Dragon, "Do you know who the host of this party is? I'm attending for someone who couldn't make it, and they forgot to mention the host's name."

Elysia was becoming more irritated that her grandmother had given her such little information.

The Faerie Dragon set down his tray of snacks on a nearby table and flew closer to Elysia "That information will cost you," he said.

Elysia was prepared for this. Almost all of the Fey, including herself occasionally, loved to bargain and make deals.

"What do you want?" Elysia asked.

"Distilled laughter of small children," he responded immediately. "In a pure crystal bottle."

Elysia sighed and reached into her pocket. She opened her extradimensional space in her pocket so the little dragon couldn't see what kind of magic she used. She pulled out an intricate crystal bottle. Inside was a swirling cloud of pastel colors. This was her last bottle of distilled laughter. She would have to pick up more later.

The little dragon grabbed the bottle from her and held it up to his face.

"This is good quality," he said. "A fine bargain. I suppose you want your information then."

He looked around and motioned her over to a more secluded corner of the room.

"The host of this gathering is Beryl of House Frost. Most of the guests are from smaller houses and could be potential allies of House Frost."

That surprised Elysia. House Frost was a relatively small family and wasn't very influential. She knew their leader was a Fey named Kraig but knew little beyond that. That explained why she hadn't recognized most of the people here. She didn't recognize the name Beryl either. House Moonwatcher was one of the most powerful families in the Unseelie Court and didn't usually interact much with the lesser houses. What had Beryl been hoping to gain by orchestrating her kidnapping and the murder of Wilfred?

"Can you point them out to me?" Elysia asked.

The dragon nodded and pointed a clawed finger at a person in the crowd. Beryl, a fairly short High Fey with short, light blue hair and dark green eyes, wore a sharp, expensive-looking suit.

Elysia had seen them when she had been spying on the people at the party. They had never seemed to be talking when she was near them, and she suspected they had somehow seen through her invisibility.

"Do you know what they hope to accomplish for their house?" Elysia asked the dragon.

The dragon narrowed his eyes at her. "I'll tell you," he said, "but I must admit that I'm interested in knowing why you're asking."

Elysia looked at him flatly. "You got your payment. Tell me."

The little dragon huffed. "Okay, okay, no need to get cranky. I don't know for certain, but rumor has it that House Frost is trying to destabilize the more influential houses to make them look weak and, in turn, make House Frost look stronger. They're tired of being unimportant and want more favor with the Queen."

That made sense to Elysia. It wasn't uncommon for smaller families to try to undermine their competition. Why had they tried to kidnap her, though? For leverage?

"That's interesting," Elysia said to the Faerie Dragon. "You're a very good informant. Will you tell me your name in case I want to make a deal with you again?"

"You can call me Loki," he said. "It was very interesting to speak with you, Elysia."

He grabbed the tray off the table and flew off, a mischievous grin on his face. Elysia was certain she hadn't told him her name. He must have recognized her. She wasn't angry at the little dragon. It was the mark of a good informant that they got more information out of the interaction than their client did. He was probably going to remember her presence at this party, as well as the specific questions she had asked.

Elysia had all the information she needed. She glanced around for Beryl but didn't see them. They were probably somewhere else in the giant tree.

Elysia walked out of the tree and around to the other side of the trunk, out of sight. On the other side of the tree was Beryl, a silver sword in their hand.

"Did you think you could crash my party without consequences," they said, "Elysia Moonwatcher?"

INTERLUDE

Zia pulled books off of the shelves. Sylvena and Malvina were still asleep, and Zia planned to stay up all night to see when Elysia returned home. She eventually got bored of sitting around and decided to go through with her plan. Zia had been planning on going through with this for a while but had never had the opportunity.

She had been looking for a specific book for an entire hour. Currently, she was looking through the part of the library that held books written by Malvina. Malvina had been on many adventures in her life and had written many books about the things she had encountered.

Finally, Zia found the book she was looking for. It was a thick book bound in red leather. The front cover had a gold title inlaid on it: *My Research and Encounters With the Demonic, written by Malvina Moonwatcher.*

This was the same book Zia had read when she was stuck in Malvina's room. The plan had begun forming in her mind that day. Zia brought the book over to a table and began looking through it. It had tips for avoiding demons, strategies for fighting them, and other useful things.

Zia found the page she was looking for. Summoning devils. She had heard that you could summon a devil and make a pact with it in exchange for power. Zia couldn't summon one in her house, which had magical protections against such things, so she grabbed the book, along with some candles, and walked outside. She walked into the woods, far enough away that she couldn't see the house anymore.

Zia set up the candles in a circle in the middle of the woods and opened the book. She read through the incantation several times. When she had memorized it, she pulled out a vial from her pocket.

The vial was full of blood. She didn't know what creature it was from. It was the same one she had stolen from Malvina a few weeks ago. Zia pulled the stopper off the bottle and poured the contents around the candles, forming a red circle in the snow. She lit the candles and spoke the incantation.

She said it in Infernal, the language of devils. She didn't know Infernal very well, but she knew enough to speak the incantation clearly. The circle flashed red as soon as she finished speaking, and all the snow inside it melted. Inside the circle, a fiery face appeared. Zia couldn't make out the features very well, but she could see that it had horns.

"Why have you summoned me," It said in a rough voice.

"I need to make a deal," Zia said, "for more power."

The creature chuckled. "I can do that in exchange for something."

Zia was prepared for this. "What do you want?" she asked.

"Give me your existing magic. It's not really that big of a request. You won't even notice it's missing. You also must gather information on your family for me. If I ask to know something about them, you must tell me what you know. In return, I will give you different magic, and you will be more powerful than you have ever imagined."

Zia briefly wondered why the devil wanted information on her family, but it didn't matter. They never told her anything important anyway. Besides, this was a good deal. Her existing magic was pathetic, and she didn't need it. She would do it if this creature were willing to make her more powerful in exchange for some light information gathering.

The ice magic Zia had inherited from her great-grandmother wasn't that powerful, and she never had any talent. Elysia had always been the talented one and the favourite. Maybe if Zia were more powerful than Elysia, she would finally get the recognition she deserved.

"I'll do it," Zia said.

Immediately, a scroll appeared in front of her. It was covered in cramped writing in Infernal. A quill appeared in her hand.

"Sign your name," the creature said. "Your true name."

Zia hesitated. All of the Fey, including herself, had a true name that held power over them. If she gave this devil her name, it could theoretically use it against her.

"Promise that you won't use my name against me," Zia said.

The creature chuckled ominously. "I would never do that," it said, "but I am getting impatient. Sign your name."

Zia picked up the scroll and signed her name.

The ink looked like blood. Immediately after she signed her name, the scroll and the quill disappeared. The creature in the circle laughed maniacally before disappearing. The candles burnt out, and Zia was left sitting in the middle of the forest, wondering if she had made a terrible mistake.

CHAPTER TEN

Elysia summoned her Shadow Blade. She had planned to leave without a fight, but Beryl apparently had other plans. Besides, she wouldn't pass up an opportunity to fight the person who had killed her father.

Beryl spoke again, "You really thought that you could waltz right in without me recognizing you? Not to mention that your attempt at invisibility was laughable."

Elysia glared at them. "You killed my father and tried to kidnap me," she said. "Why? For some stupid ploy to get your family more renown?"

"I didn't kill your father. And I didn't even organize his death. He was collateral damage. I told those ignorant humans that as long as they brought you back, they could get rid of the vampire as they wished."

Elysia was furious. "It wouldn't have even mattered! My family would have crushed your house once they figured out what was happening."

Beryl shrugged. "They could have. They also could not have. I was willing to take the risk for my family. Your house had too much power, and the smaller houses like mine were being forgotten. Someone needed to do something."

Elysia pointed her blade toward them. "You won't get away with this. Even if I don't make it out of here, my grandmother will destroy you."

Beryl lifted their sword. "Are you even going to fight me? Or do you just want to stand here all night chit-chatting?"

In response, shadows shot up from the ground around Elysia, twisting toward Beryl. Beryl dodged out of the way, running over to Elysia. They swung their sword at her. She barely managed to get out of the way. Beryl was a much better fighter than the humans Elysia had fought. She was actually excited to have a skilled opponent for once.

Elysia stepped away from Beryl. They hadn't been very smart to pick a fight with her at night when everything was in darkness. Elysia pulled the shadows around Beryl, briefly distracting them. They stumbled briefly, and Elysia landed a hit on their arm.

They cursed and spun around, swiping at Elysia and slicing some of the fabric of her dress. Elysia stepped back out of their reach, calling on her shadows to make her invisible. Let them see her 'laughable' technique now.

Beryl tried to attack the spot where Elysia had just been standing, and she quickly moved closer to strike. Beryl must have anticipated her actions because they quickly moved their blade to parry her attack.

Elysia stepped out of Beryl's reach, melting into the shadow of a nearby tree. She quietly crept around the edge of the forest. She jumped out from behind Beryl, but they twisted at the last second, and Elysia stumbled.

She was stunned for a moment. Had she just made a *mistake?* It had been years since she had made such an obvious blunder. Was Beryl more skilled than she had thought at first? As Elysia tried to regain her footing, Beryl swung their blade at her. It hit Elysia in the side, and she barely managed to get out of the way before Beryl could attack her again.

Elysia quickly ran back to the tree cover, becoming invisible again and sitting down on the ground. She looked at her wound. It wasn't deep or very life-threatening, but it *hurt. Well,* she thought, *at least it isn't an iron blade.*

One of the only benefits of fighting another Fey versus a human was that they didn't use iron weapons. If she had to guess, Beryl's sword was likely made of adamantine or a similar, non-toxic metal. Even with Elysia's newfound resistance to iron, she was still weakened by it, and if she had to choose, she would much rather die to a normal weapon than an iron one.

Elysia watched Beryl. They were slowly walking around the forest's edge, trying to find her hiding spot. Elysia briefly debated leaving. Beryl hadn't found where she was hidden yet, and she could probably sneak away and then call her grandmother to bring her home. But she didn't *want* to leave. She had to finish this fight. She *could* defeat Beryl. Probably. Besides, she couldn't return to her grandmother and say she had failed.

With newfound resolve, Elysia stood up and looked at Beryl. They had gotten closer and were only about two yards away now. Elysia remembered something her father had told her. "*When you're fighting against a skilled opponent, sometimes the only way to win is to wait for them to make a mistake. And if they don't make mistakes, then you have to improvise.*"

Elysia stepped out from behind a tree to Beryl's side a minute later, and they spun around.

"Not dead yet, I see," they said, slowly walking towards her.

"You can't get rid of me that easily," Elysia replied. She just needed them to walk a little closer and…

As Beryl stepped beneath the shadow of a large conifer, a massive nest of shadowy tendrils shot down on them. The trap that Elysia had set a moment before activating. They tried to dodge to the side, but more tendrils of darkness reached out from behind the nearby trees, encasing them in a web of shadowy tentacles. Beryl struggled for a moment before realizing that it was pointless.

Elysia walked forward, her shadow blade materializing her hand. She paused in front of Beryl.

"What are you waiting for?" Beryl said. "Go ahead. Kill me. Get your revenge."

Elysia was silent for a long moment, staring at Beryl. She could kill them. She could finally get the revenge that she had been waiting for.

"No," Elysia said.

Beryl looked surprised. "What?"

"I'm not going to kill you."

"Then you're an idiot," Beryl said. "You've grown up in the Winter Court, same as me. You let me live, and you're going to regret it."

"No, I won't. I'm going to let you go," Elysia said, "on one condition. Leave my family alone. I don't care who else you try to undermine, but leave my family out of it."

Elysia had realized something as the fight progressed. She didn't want to kill Beryl. She wasn't filled with murderous intent, looking forward to causing destruction. She just wanted to *win*. And she had to admit to herself she just wanted her father back. It wasn't fair that he had died. But that wasn't going to happen. He was dead, and killing Beryl wasn't going to change that, no matter how much she wanted it to. It was Beryl's fault, but she could see where they came from. They weren't so different from Elysia, in a way. They just wanted a better life for their family. That didn't excuse their actions, but it wasn't necessarily a reason to kill them.

"And why would I do that?" Beryl said.

Elysia looked them straight in the eyes. "Because if you don't, I will crush your family. I will make sure that every one of them dies, but not before I take all of the resources you have and destroy your reputation. Then I will find out where you live, and I will kill you. Not at first, I'll let you lose some sleep over the fact you don't know when I'm coming and that it was your fault that your family suffered. And I'll make sure you never even have a chance to fight back."

Elysia smiled at them, all seriousness gone from her voice. "But if you leave my family alone, none of that has to happen, right?"

Beryl looked unnerved. Elysia had that effect on people sometimes.

"Fine," they said, "leave before I change my mind."

Elysia sighed. Even though they were at an extreme disadvantage, they still acted like they held all the leeway.

"Do you swear to hold to your word and make no moves against House Moonwatcher?" Elysia asked.

Beryl sighed. "I swear," they said.

That was good enough for Elysia. She knew that Beryl could tell no lies, and their promise was good enough for her. Elysia turned to walk into the forest but paused and turned around to speak to Beryl again.

"Fun party, by the way," Elysia said before the shadows crept around her and she disappeared, leaving Beryl alone in the woods.

Elysia quickly ran into the forest. She stopped when she was about ten yards away from Beryl. She dismissed the shadows that had been restraining them. They appeared mostly unruffled but extremely annoyed. She watched to see what they would do now that she was gone. She was certain that Beryl would keep their word, but nothing in their agreement said they couldn't follow her.

Beryl looked around for a few seconds, shook their head, and walked back around the tree. Elysia waited a minute, then set off into the night. She was quite proud of what she had accomplished that night. She had found out who had killed her father, gotten information on House Frost, and discouraged Beryl from going after her family again.

She hadn't been bluffing when she had talked about destroying House Frost. Her family was much more powerful and could crush them easily. She had also just proven that she could beat Beryl in a fight. She hadn't seen Beryl use much magic other than seeing through her invisibility, which meant that they either didn't use it on purpose or didn't have much that was useful in direct combat.

After walking for about five minutes, Elysia stopped. She didn't see anything in the nearby area, but that didn't mean there wasn't anything or anyone around. The Feywild, especially the Unseelie Court, was a very dangerous place. You never knew what could be following or watching you.

It was the dead of night, almost the Witching Hour. Elysia's shadow magic was strongest at night. She pulled the shadows in a ten-by-ten-foot circle around her, creating a physical barrier that should also prevent anyone from seeing inside with magic. It was time to call her grandmother.

Her grandmother hadn't specified how she would contact Elysia or even if she would. Elysia knew it was dangerous to draw her attention without being specifically instructed, but Elysia needed to speak with her.

Elysia took a deep breath and said, "Grandmother, I need to talk to you."

Nothing happened. That was expected. Most Archfey and other powerful beings only responded when you called their name three times.

"Illiyith," Elysia said again, "Illiyith Moonwatcher, I need to speak with you."

She waited for a few seconds and was about to try again when she heard her great-grandmother's voice from behind her. "You did well, Elysia. Tell me what you found."

Elysia spun around and saw her grandmother standing behind her, leaning on her ice crystal staff.

"I'm glad you came," Elysia said. "Will we be overheard?"

Illiyith looked around. "No. You did a good job with the barrier. Your skill has improved in the last few decades. Now, what did you discover?"

"House Frost is trying to undermine us. One of their members, Beryl, was the person who tried to kidnap me and had my father killed. House Frost is trying to gain more influence and power. I fought Beryl, and they agreed to leave us alone in exchange for us not crushing their house." Elysia paused for a moment. "Of course, I didn't agree that *we* would leave *them* alone, so we can still destroy them if we need to."

Illiyith smiled at her. "You did very well indeed, and you passed my test. I wanted to see if you could find this out by yourself, and you even managed to fix the problem."

Elysia was delighted. She could scarcely believe the things she had accomplished in such a short period of time. And to have her grandmother be so proud of her was the best outcome she could have hoped for.

"I'm glad I was able to succeed," Elysia said. "I knew I wouldn't let you down." She hesitated for a moment. "If it's not too much trouble, do you think you could bring me back home? I forgot to bring a means of transportation."

Illiyith walked over to Elysia and put her hand on her shoulder. They vanished from the forest, leaving no trace that they had ever been there.

CHAPTER ELEVEN

Illiyith had teleported Elysia directly in front of Elysia's house. Illiyith turned to Elysia, looking at her. She waved her hand, and all of Elysia's injuries vanished, including the gash on her side. That was good because Elysia felt a little dizzy from blood loss.

Illiyith smiled and then disappeared, leaving Elysia alone. Elysia was surprised that she had healed her. Apparently, Illiyith was feeling generous today.

Elysia walked up to the house and stepped inside. The door wouldn't open for anyone who wasn't a family member, so Elysia didn't need to worry about locking it.

It was almost three in the morning, and her family would all be asleep. She crept up the stairs to her room. She quietly shut the door behind her.

"Where were you, Elysia?" she heard a voice say.

Elysia turned around in surprise. She saw Zia standing behind her, arms crossed. Elysia saw Nyx behind her, sleeping on a pillow on Elysia's bed.

"Were you waiting in my room this entire time, Zia?"

"Tell me where you went," Zia said.

"I told you already, I went to a party. You weren't invited."

Zia didn't look convinced but dropped the subject. As she walked past Elysia to the door, Elysia held out a hand to stop her.

"What's going on, Zia?" Elysia said. "You seem different."

As soon as she saw Zia, she noticed something off about her. She didn't know what, but something was different. Zia seemed… darker. Not just the cranky younger sister that Elysia knew. Something had definitely changed, but Elysia couldn't quite tell what it was.

"I'm fine, Elysia," Zia said. "Actually, I'm better than ever. You've gotten too used to being the most powerful one of us, Elysia. Maybe I've just gotten better in the time you've been gone."

Then she stepped around Elysia and left the room, closing the door behind her. As she left, Elysia thought she caught a flash of red in Zia's normally silver eyes. It could have been a trick of the light, but maybe not.

"What are you up to, Zia?" she whispered when Zia was gone.

Elysia walked over and sat down next to Nyx. The little Displacer Beast was snoring softly. Even though Elysia had found out who had orchestrated her father's death, proved herself to her grandmother, and adopted a dangerous cat, she felt like she had more questions than ever.

What secret was Zia keeping? Why was House Frost challenging the balance of power now? What were her grandmother's plans?

Elysia picked up Nyx and set her in her lap. Nyx stared at her, tail swishing, annoyed that Elysia had woken her up.

"I don't know what my sister's up to," Elysia said, "and I don't know what's going on in the Court, but we're going to find out together."

Nyx meowed resolutely and curled up in a ball, purring. Even if Elysia couldn't trust her sister, at least she still had her cat.

ABOUT THE AUTHOR

Tressym is the author of *Shadows of the Past*, her debut novel. She enjoys reading fantasy books and playing Dungeons & Dragons when she's not writing. She also serves as the editor of *Luna Magazine*. Tressym resides in northern Minnesota with her cats and other beloved pets.